PiGGie Pie!

by **Margie Palatini** • Illustrated by **Howard Fine**

SCHOLASTIC INC. • New York Toronto London Auckland Sydney

ISBN 0-590-12702-0

Text copyright © 1995 by Margie Palatini.
Illustrations copyright © 1995 by Howard Fine.
All rights reserved. Published by Scholastic Inc., 555 Broadway, New York, NY 10012,
by arrangement with Clarion Books, a Houghton Mifflin Company imprint.

SCHOLASTIC and associated logos are trademarks and/or registered trademarks
of Scholastic Inc.

12 11 10 9 8 7 6 5 4 3 2 1   7 8 9/9 0 1 2/0

Printed in the U.S.A.   08

First Scholastic printing, September 1997

For Jamie, my one and only.
—M.P.

To my wife, Rona, for her patience, love, and support.
—H.F.

ritch the Witch woke up grouchy, grumpy, and very hungry.
Her belly grumbled for something delicious.
Something delightful.
Something special.
  But what?
It wasn't purple mouse-tail stew.
No, she ate that yesterday for lunch.
Maybe some mashed dragon-tongue pudding?
No. Gritch wasn't in the mood for anything quite that sweet.
Perhaps a taste of boiled black buzzard feet?
That always made her mouth water.
  No, not today.
Today Gritch wanted something truly tasty.
Something really yummy.
Something SPECIAL!
And that could only mean . . .

"Yes, yes, Piggie Pie!
I can taste those plump, juicy, pink piggies
right now," Gritch said, smacking her lips.

She hurried to the pantry and pulled
down her *Old Hag Cookbook* from the
top shelf. She picked off a spider, blew off
the dust, and turned to the secret recipe
on page 342. Gritch ran her bony finger
with the long green nail down the list of
ingredients.

1 eye of a fly
She checked the pantry shelves.
"No problem," said Gritch.
2 shakes of a rattlesnake's rattle
"No problem," said Gritch.
3 belly hairs of a possum
"No problem," said Gritch.
8 plump piggies

"**Problem!**

screeched Gritch.
"I don't have any piggies!
How can I make Piggie Pie
without even one puny pink pig?"
Gritch pulled her hair.
She stomped her feet.
She paced the floor.
She wanted Piggie Pie.
She wanted Piggie Pie very much!
  "Hmmm," she said,
tapping the lucky wart on her chin.
"Now where would I find
eight plump pigs?"

Gritch thought. And thought. And thought.
"Aha!" she shouted with a jump.
"The circus! Yes, yes, the circus!

The CIRCUS? No, no, not the circus.
You don't find pigs in the circus."
　She thought harder.
"Aha!" she shouted with a jump.
"The zoo! Yes, yes, the zoo!
The ZOO? No, no, not the zoo.
You don't find pigs in the zoo."
　She thought much harder.
"The FARM? Yes! Yes! The farm!
You find pigs on the farm."
There still was just one teeny, tiny, little PROBLEM . . .
where to find a farm. "WHERE ELSE?" Gritch let her bony fingers do the walking
and opened the Yellow Pages to F, where she found a very large ad.
　THIS WAS IT!

Gritch put her broomstick in gear
and headed over the river and through the woods to Old MacDonald's farm.

"I've got you in my sights now, you little porkers!" she cackled as she circled overhead.

Gritch zoomed in for a **THUMP-P-P! THUMP-P-P! ERRRRCH-CH!** landing.
She spit straw, fanned her still-smoking tootsies, and lifted her goggles.
There wasn't a pig in sight!
"Where did they all go?" Gritch shouted to a duck.
"Hey, duck! I said, where are all the piggies?
I need eight plump piggies for Piggie Pie."
The duck quack-quacked here.
It quack-quacked there.
Here it quacked.
There it quacked.
Everywhere it quack-quacked, "No piggies."

"What do you mean, *no piggies*,
you dizzy duck?" Gritch screeched into
his bill. "I just saw a passel of piggies
down here not a minute ago! Hand
over those hogs, you little quacker."

"No piggies," quacked the duck.
Gritch pulled her hair.
She stomped her feet.
She even threatened the duck
with one of her most evil spells.

The duck was not impressed.
It wasn't even scared.
It gave Gritch another quack
and waddled away.

"So, who needs a dumb duck?"
Gritch mumbled.

Being careful where she stepped, Gritch wandered across the meadow.

"Yoo hoo," she shouted.

"Moo?"

"You," Gritch said to the cow. "Where are the piggies?
I need eight plump piggies for Piggie Pie."

The cow moo-mooed here.

It moo-mooed there.

Here it mooed.

There it mooed.

Everywhere it moo-mooed, "No piggies."

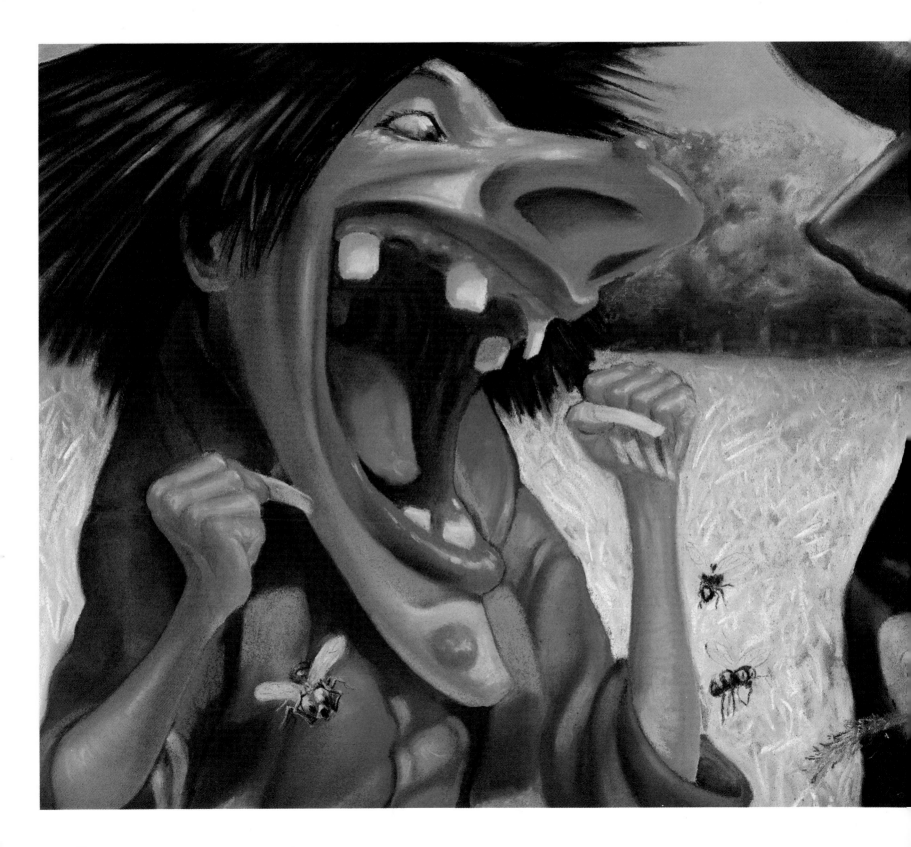

"What do you mean, *no piggies,*
you lumpy-looking cow!" screamed Gritch.
"I need eight plump piggies for Piggie Pie!
Fork over the pork, you walking milk
machine, or I'll curdle your cream!"
    "No piggies," mooed the cow.
Gritch pulled her hair.
She stomped her feet.
She even threatened the cow
with one of her most evil spells.
    The cow stared at Gritch,
swatted a fly with its tail,
and lumbered away.
    "Cows! Who needs 'em?" Gritch muttered.

So she tried the barnyard, where she stopped a chicken in its tracks.
"Okay, birdbrain. Where are the piggies?
I need eight plump piggies for Piggie Pie."
The chicken cluck-clucked here.
It cluck-clucked there.
Here it clucked.
There it clucked.
Everywhere it cluck-clucked, "No piggies."

"What do you mean, *no piggies*, you feathered drumstick?" Gritch screeched. "What's going on here? Where's the boss of this heap of hay?" The chicken flapped a wing toward Old MacDonald.

Gritch looked him over once. Twice.

"You're Old MacDonald?" she said. "Don't look much like your picture, do you?"

The farmer thumbed his suspenders and shrugged.

"Look, Shorty, I've been quack-quacked here, moo-mooed there, and cluck-clucked everywhere all over this farm. I need eight plump piggies for Piggie Pie. Where are the piggies?"

The farmer looked here. He looked there. Here he looked. There he looked. Everywhere he looked and looked. "No piggies."

"What do you mean, *no piggies?* You flea-bitten seed spreader! You *must* have piggies!"
Gritch pulled her hair. She stomped her feet.
She even threatened him with one of her most evil spells.

"No piggies!"

Her stomach growled. It grumbled. But there were no piggies. There would be no Piggie Pie.
Now what was she going to eat?

"Psst . . . psst . . . PSSST! . . . Excuse me, little lady.
Wolf's the name.
Let me give you some advice.
Forget about the pigs."
   "Forget about the pigs?" said Gritch, eyeing the wolf.
   He nodded. "They're too tricky. Trust me.
I've been chasing three little pigs for days."
He huffed and puffed.
"I'm starving. Look at me. I'm nothing but skin and bones!"

Gritch pinched his arm. "Well, not quite." She grinned.

"Mr. Wolf, I have the most wonderful idea. I was thinking, since you haven't eaten, and I haven't eaten, why don't you come home with me for lunch? I'm a very good cook."

"Why, that does sound tempting," the wolf said as he looked at Gritch and smacked his lips.

"Are you sure it wouldn't be any problem?"

"PROBLEM?" Gritch grinned.

"No problem at all," she said as they walked off arm in arm.
"I always enjoy having a wolf for lunch."